BOOK 2

ACCENT ON ACCENTS

BY **ELLIOT FINE** *and* **MARVIN DAHLGREN**

AF348705

TABLE OF CONTENTS

INTRODUCTION

This book is written in the contemporary notation.   This means that instead of using a musical staff when we write for snare drum as in figure 1

we simplify it by using a single line as in figure 2.

When the note heads are written on the line (figure 3), any sticking may be used.   However, you will find that, in most cases, alternate sticking (RLRL) or (LRLR) is the most practical.

In order to gain the most proficiency, practice starting with the left hand as much as you practice starting with the right hand.

When it is desirable to indicate the sticking in an exercise, the note heads will be written above and below the line.   Notes written above the line are to be played with the right hand (study figure 4).

Figure 4 would be played as 8 consecutive right hands.

Notes written below the line (as in figure 5) are to be played with the left hand.

Figure 5 would be played as 8 consecutive left hands.

Alternate sticking is written as in figure 6.

Figure 6 is played RLRL RLRL.

A single paradiddle, which in the old notation would be written as in figure 7A, will be written in the contemporary style as in figure 7B

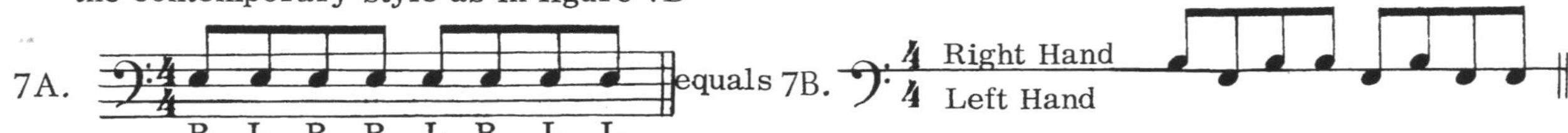

The advantages of the contemporary notation are:

I. The rhythm and the sticking become one. In other words, they are comprehended at the same time.

II. The exact rhythm of each hand (or limb) is easier to see. This makes it possible to practice each hand (or limb) separately in order to correct any deficiencies.

III. A short hand system is possible, which makes writing sticking exercises faster and which may be used as a supplement to ordinary notation. (This will be explained later in the book).

IV. By assigning different limbs to the upper and lower notes, each exercise may be practiced 8 different ways.

1. As an exercise for the hands.
2. As an exercise for the feet.
3. As an exercise for the right hand and right foot.
4. As an exercise for the left hand and left foot.
5. As an exercise for the right hand and left foot.
6. As an exercise for the left hand and right foot.
7. As an exercise for both hands and both feet.
8. As a musical exercise for two tom toms or timpani.

To become better acquainted with the contemporary style of writing, practice the following simple exercises:

LONG ROLL: 8.

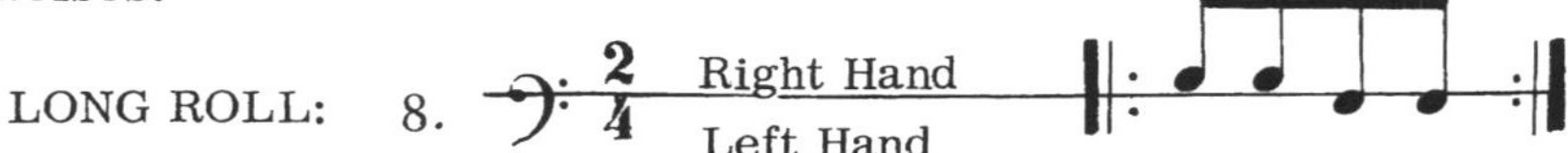

Figure 8 is two rights, two lefts. Play: (Right; right; left; left.)

Single Paradiddle:

9.

Figure 9 (Single Paradiddle) is one right; one left; two rights; one left; one right; two lefts.
Play (RLRR LRLL).

1st inversion Single Paradiddle:

10.

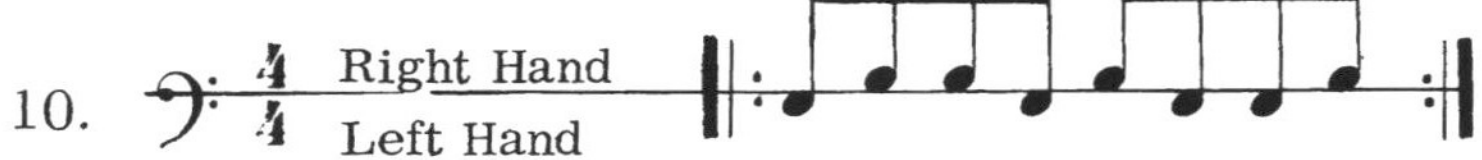

Figure 10 is one left; two rights; one left; one right; two lefts; one right. Play (LRRL RLLR).

2nd inversion Single Paradiddle:

11.

Figure 11 is two rights; one left; one right; two lefts; one right; one left. Play (RRLR LLRL).

3rd inversion Single Paradiddle:

12. 

Figure 12 is one right; one left; one right; two lefts; one right; one left; one right. Play (RLRL LRLR).

THE FOLLOWING TERMS ARE USED BY THE AUTHORS:

HIGH POSITION - Tip of stick points straight up.

MEDIUM POSITION - Stick at approximately 45 to 60 degree angle from drum.

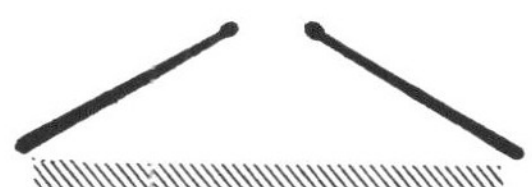

LOW POSITION - Tip of stick 4 to 6 inches off drum.

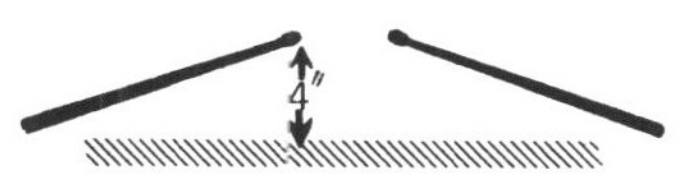

SINGLE STROKE - A single blow played by one hand.

DOUBLE STROKE - Two blows played by one hand.

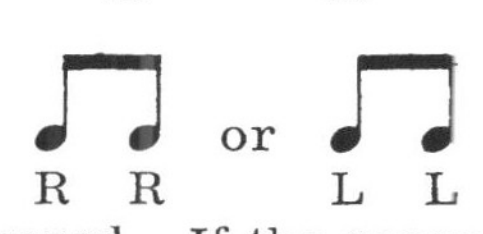

At fast speeds the second blow is bounced. If the second note of a double stroke is accented, it is snapped down by the fingers. This action is a simple one, consisting of closing the fingers on the palm of the hand. It is the precise timing of this action that is apt to give trouble.

TRIPLE STROKE - Three blows played by one hand. At fast speeds, the second and third blows are bounced.

DOWN STROKE - An accented single stroke. Start in high position; play stroke, and stop in low position. It may also start in medium position and stop in low position.

FULL STROKE - An accented single stroke. Start in high position; play stroke, and stop in high position. It may also start and stop in medium position.

UP STROKE - An unaccented single stroke. Start in low position; play stroke, and stop in high position. It may also start in low position and stop in medium position.

TAP - An unaccented single stroke. Start in low position; play stroke, and stop in low position.

A "d" under a note indicates down stroke.

An "f" under a note indicates full stroke.

A "u" under a note indicates an upstroke.

A "t" under a note indicates a tap.

For experience in reading accents in the contemporary notation, practice the following single hand exercises. R. H. = Right Hand.

RIGHT HAND EXERCISES

(Four 8th Notes)

Example: No. 1 is: right hand downstroke; right hand tap; right hand tap; right hand upstroke.

RIGHT HAND EXERCISES

(Three 8th Notes)

Example: No. 16 is: right hand downstroke; right hand tap; right hand upstroke.

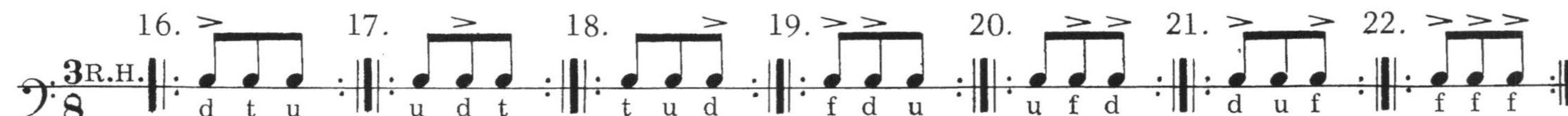

Note: It is permissable to allow the elbow to swing out in a relaxed manner to a position about 8" from the body on any stroke immediately preceding the upstroke.

For experience in reading accents in the contemporary notation, practice the following single hand exercises. L. H. = Left Hand.

LEFT HAND EXERCISES

(Four 8th Notes)

Example: No. 1 is: left hand downstroke; left hand tap; left hand tap; left hand upstroke.

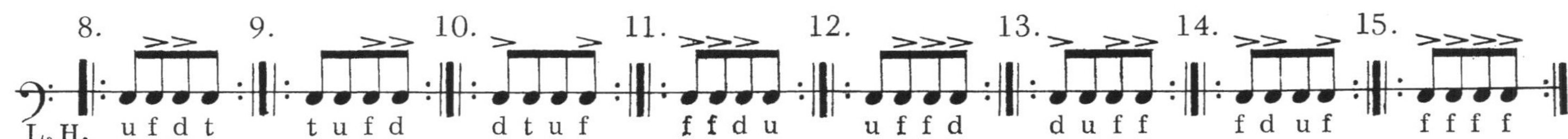

LEFT HAND EXERCISES

(Three 8th Notes)

Example: No. 16 is: left hand downstroke; left hand tap; left hand upstroke.

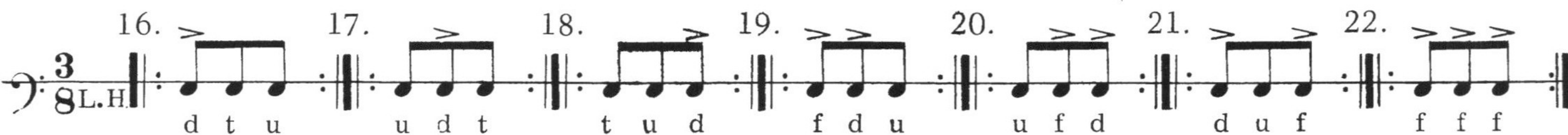

Note: It is permissable to allow the elbow to swing out in a relaxed manner to a position about 8" from the body on any stroke immediately preceding the upstroke.

ADDING THE FEET

When we wish to add the feet to an exercise, instead of using a musical staff as in figure 1

we simplify it by using a single line written below the snare drum line as in figure 2.

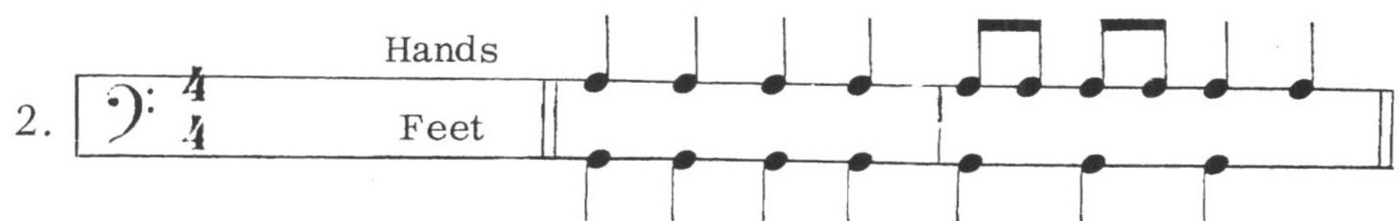

When the note heads are written on the bottom line, either foot may be used.

When the note heads are written above the bottom line, it means to play them with the right foot.

When the note heads are written below the bottom lines, it means to play them with the left foot.

R. F. = Right Foot   R. H. = Right Hand
L. F. = Left Foot   L. F. = Left Hand

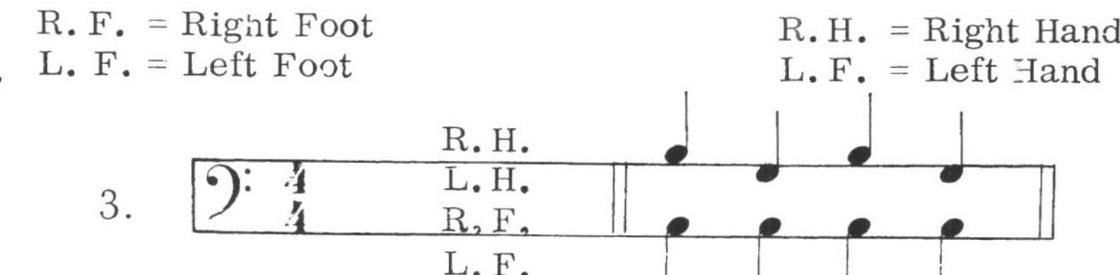

In figure 3 the notes above the bottom line indicate 4 consecutive right feet.

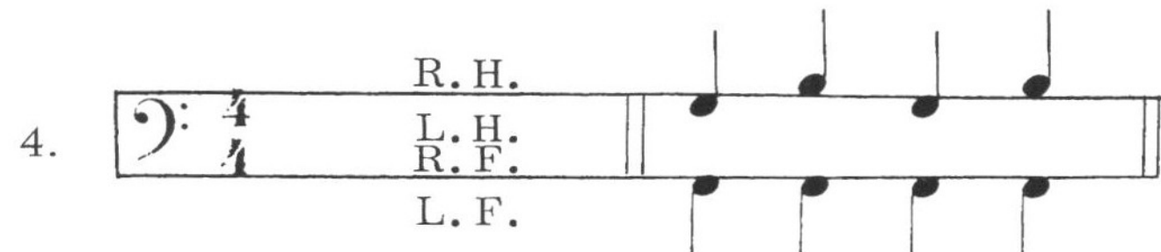

In figure 4 the notes below the bottom line indicate 4 consecutive left feet.

When the feet are used to maintain a steady rhythm (in other words, when playing the beat), we write the stems of the foot notes down.

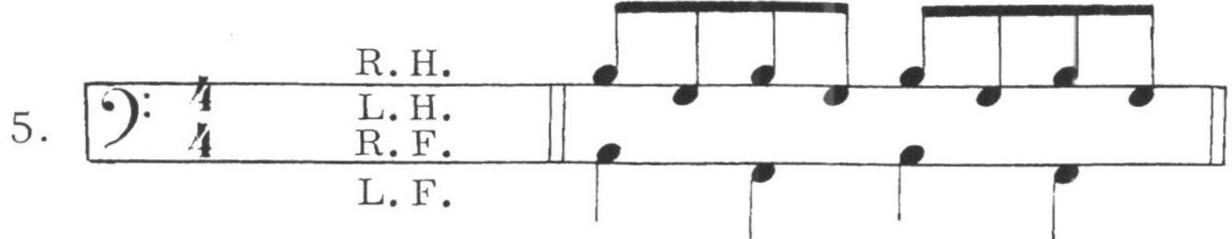

In this example (fig. 5), both the hands and the feet are alternating (RLRL), but the hands are playing 8th notes, the feet are playing quarter notes. In other words, the hands are playing twice as fast.

In some cases, especially when the feet are used in a syncopated manner, we write the stems of the foot notes up and connect them to the note heads for the hands. This shows the placement of the feet in relation to the hands more clearly.

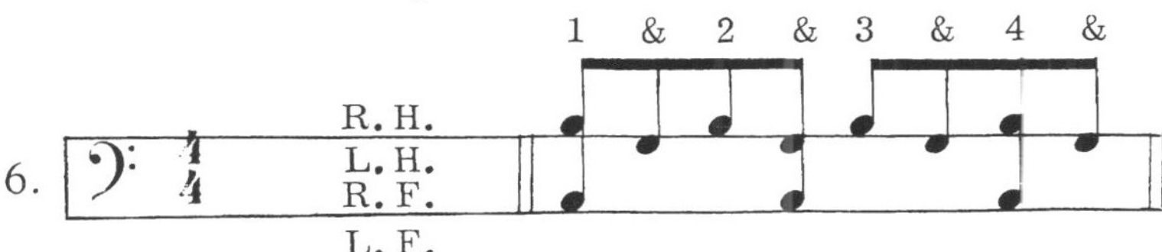

In this example (fig. 6), the right foot plays with the right hand on 1 - with the left hand on the after beat of 2 - with the right hand on 4.

NOTE TO CONCERT DRUMMERS: Please do not think that because we add the feet to the exercises in this book it is a book only for drum set players. The feet must be added for the jazz drummer, but the exercises in this book may be played by the hands alone. Indeed, this book will benefit the concert drummer as much as the jazz drummer.

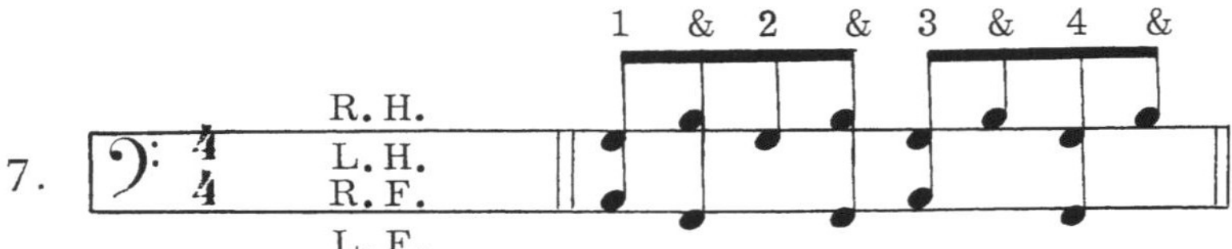

In this example (fig.7), the right foot plays with the left hand on 1; the left foot with the right hand on the after beat of 1; the left foot with the right hand on the after beat of 2; the right foot with the left hand on 3; the left foot with the left hand on 4.

If both hands are to be played simultaneously, both the note heads above and below the top line are written:

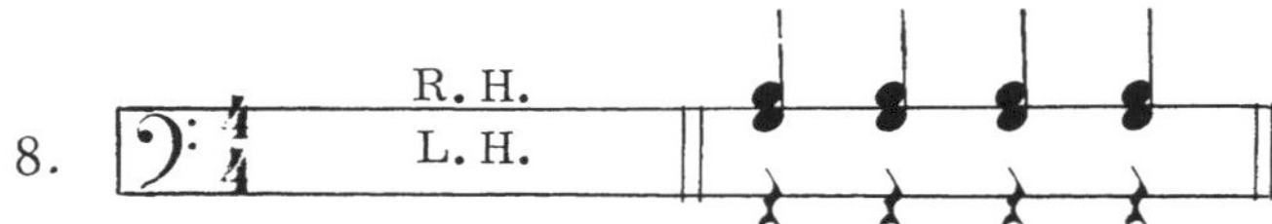

In figure 8, both hands play four consecutive notes.

If both feet are to be played simultaneously, both the note heads above and below the bottom line are written:

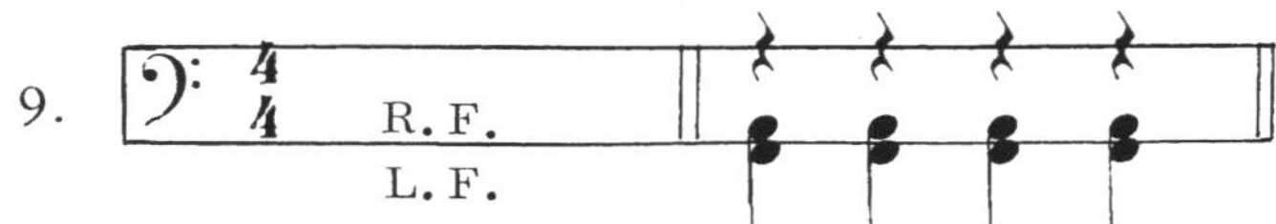

In figure 9, both feet play four consecutive notes.

ADDING ACCENTS:

Accent marks are normally written above the stems of the notes to be accented.

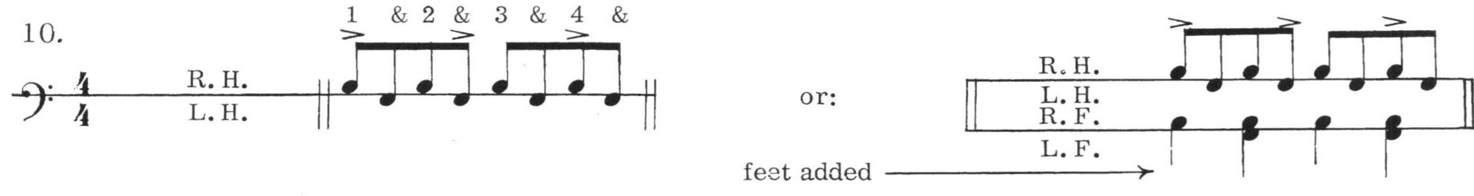

The only exception is when both hands are played simultaneously. Then the right hand note will have its accent mark above the stem; the left hand note will have its accent mark below the note head.

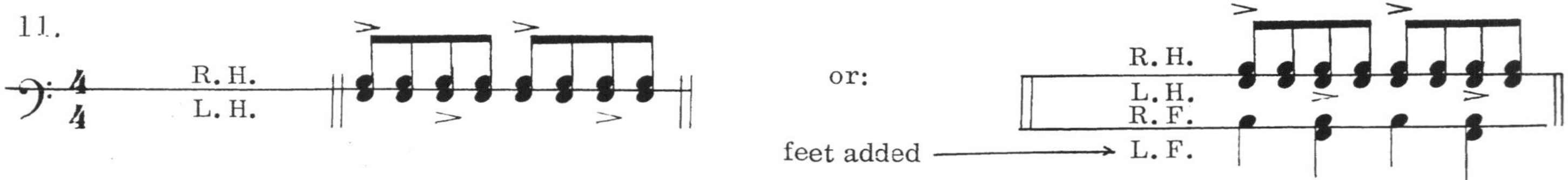

In figure 11, accent right hand on 1 and 3; accent left hand on 2 and 4.

COMBINATIONS AND SEQUENCES OF ACCENTS

Accenting every 3rd note in two measure phrases.

1. Practice in two measure phrases. 2. Practice in eight measure phrases.

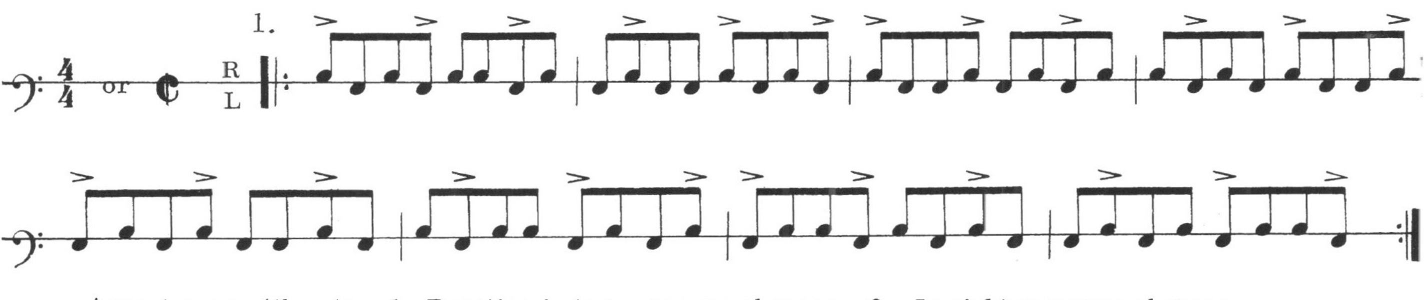

Accent every 4th note. 1. Practice in two measure phrases. 2. In eight measure phrases.

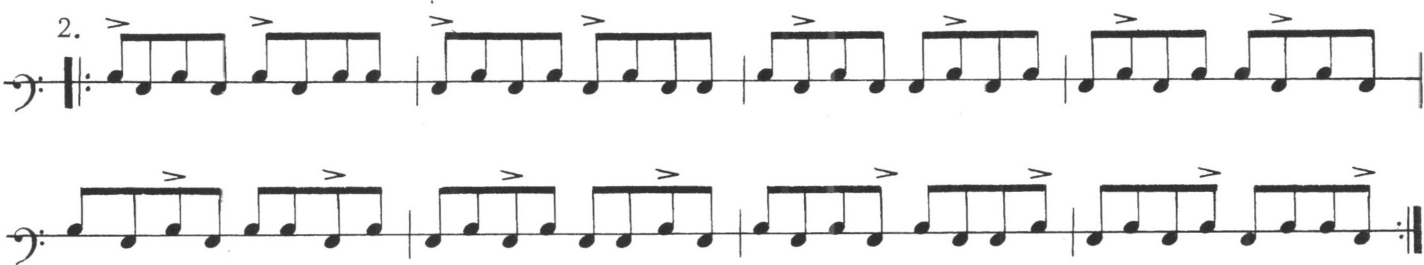

Accent every 5th note. 1. Practice in four measure phrases. 2. In eight measure phrases.

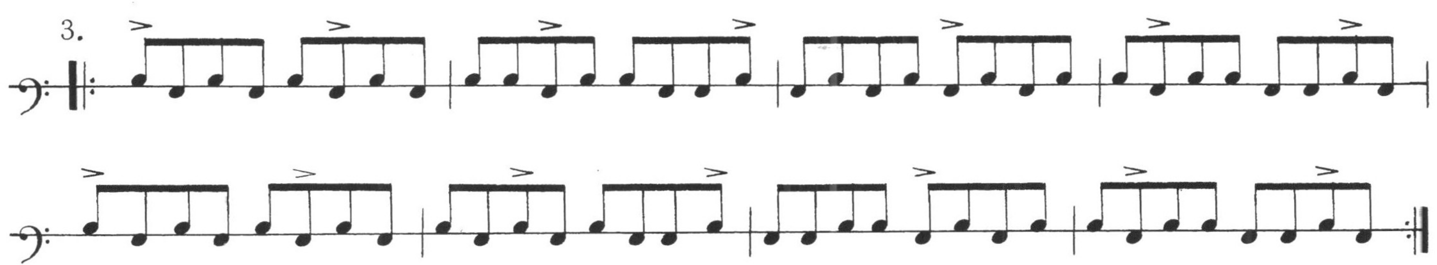

Accent every 3rd note. 1. Two measure phrases. 2. Eight measure phrases.

3rd and 4th sequence.

Accent every 4th note.

Accent every 5th note.

Accent every 6th note.   Accent every 7th.

3rd, 4th, 5th sequence.   5th, 4th, 3rd sequence.

MIRROR EXERCISES
(2nd half of exercise is opposite 1st half)

11
7.
3 3 3 3
simile
8.
9.
10.
11.
12.
13.
14.
R.
L.
4/4
HAB 104

MIRROR EXERCISES
1.
simile
2.
simile
3.
simile
4.
simile
5.
simile
6.
simile
7.
8.
9.
10.
11.
12.

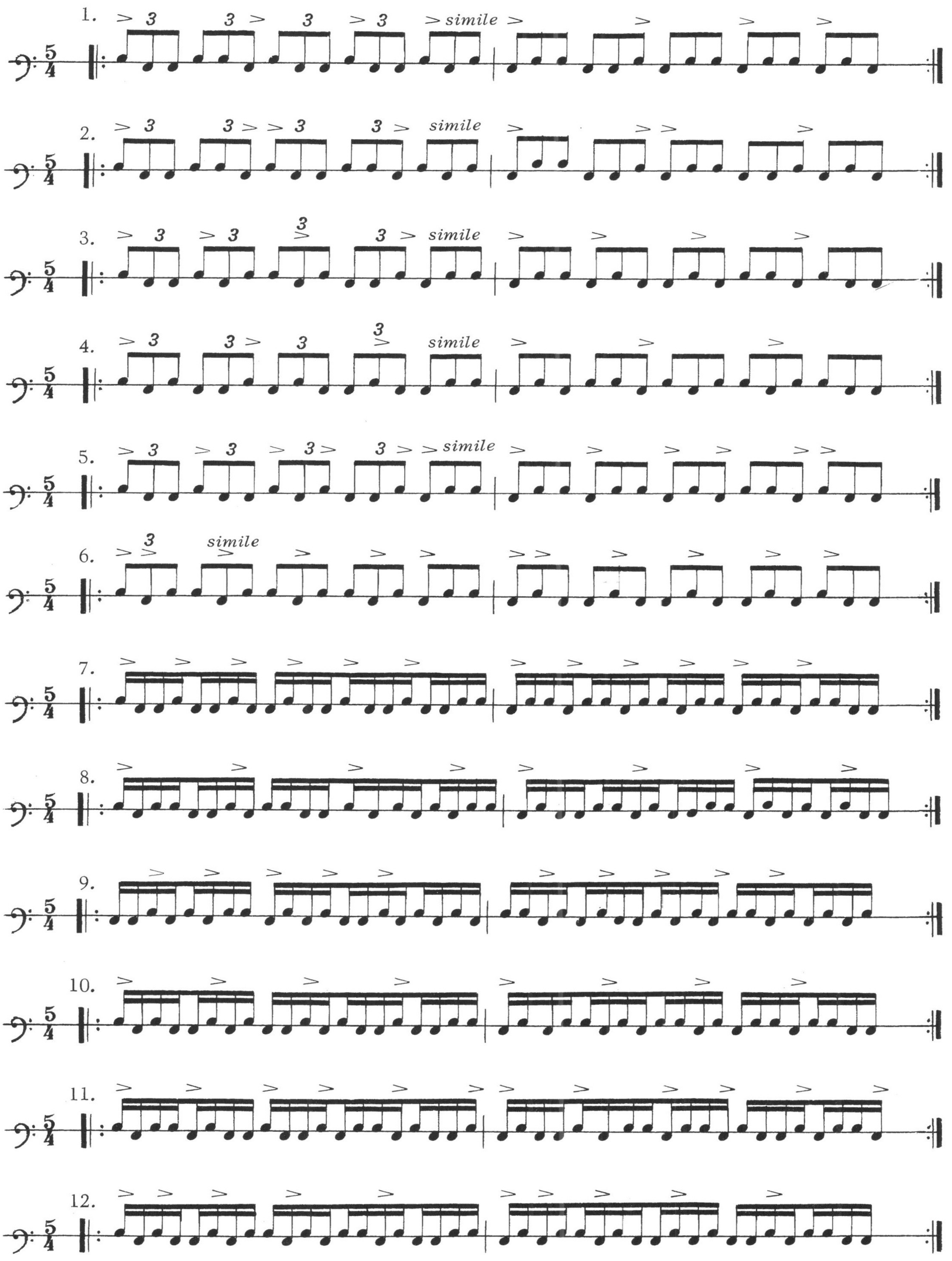

HAB 104

SINGLE HAND ACCENT STUDIES

RIGHT HAND ACCENTING (left hand playing single stroke fill)

Single accent; double accent   s = single accent   d = double accent

LEFT HAND ACCENTING (right hand playing single stroke fill)

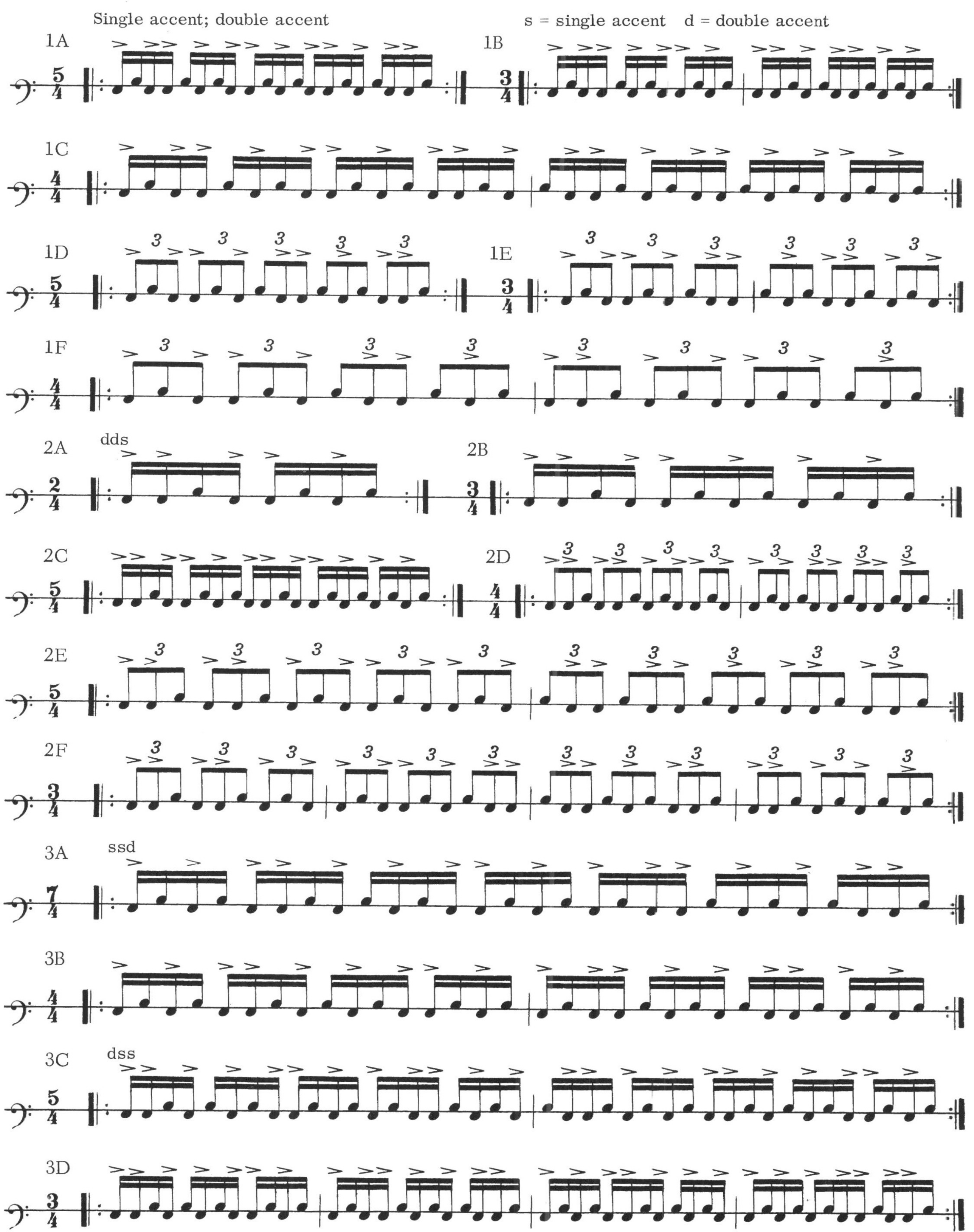

3E sds 7/4
3F 3/4
3G ssd 4/4
3H dss 5/4
4A sdds 5/4   4B 3/4
4C dssd 4/4
4D 5/4
4E ddss 3/4
4F 4/4
5 sdss 9/4
6A 3/4   6B 5/4

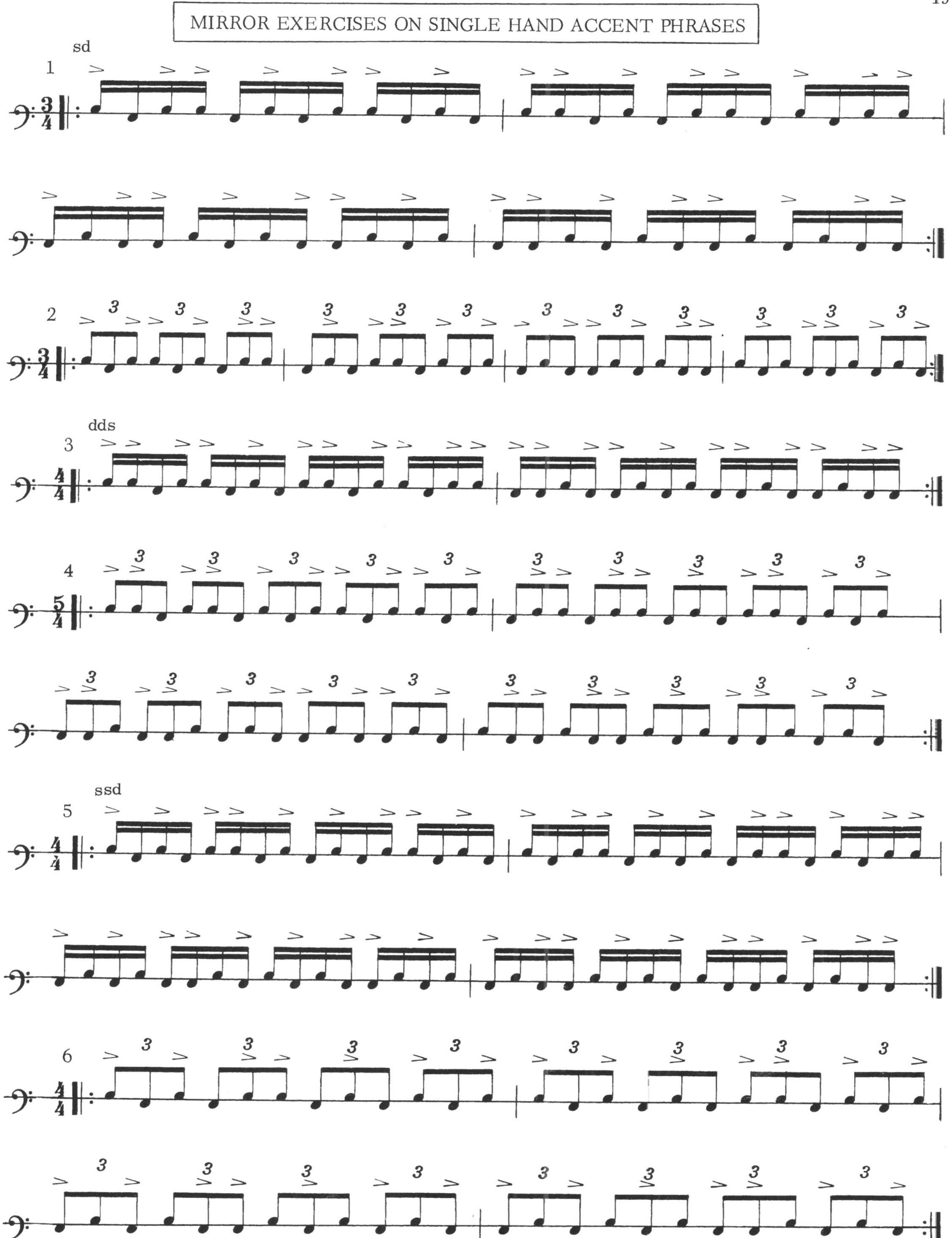

MIRROR EXERCISES ON SINGLE HAND ACCENT PHRASES
sd
1
2
dds
3
4
ssd
5
6

7
dssd 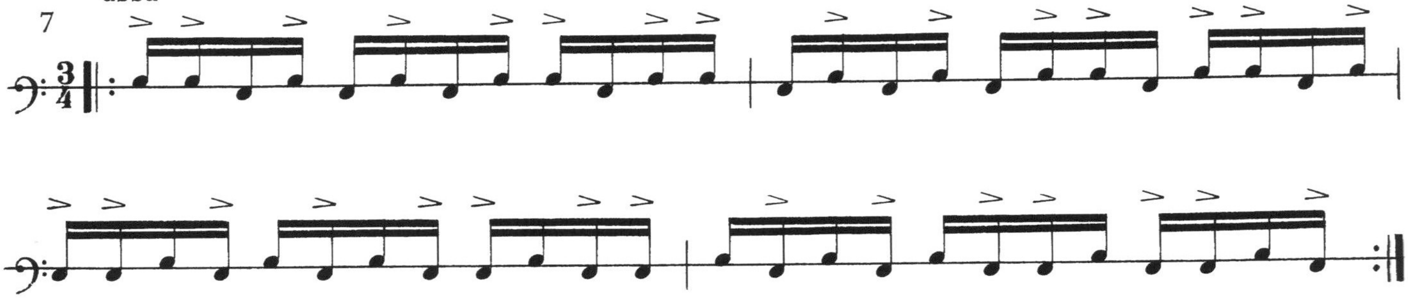
3/4
8 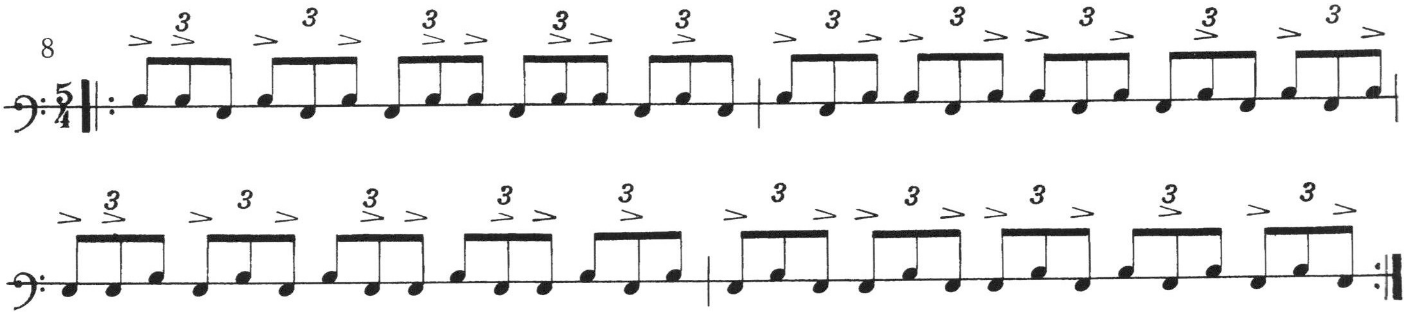
5/4
3
9
sssd 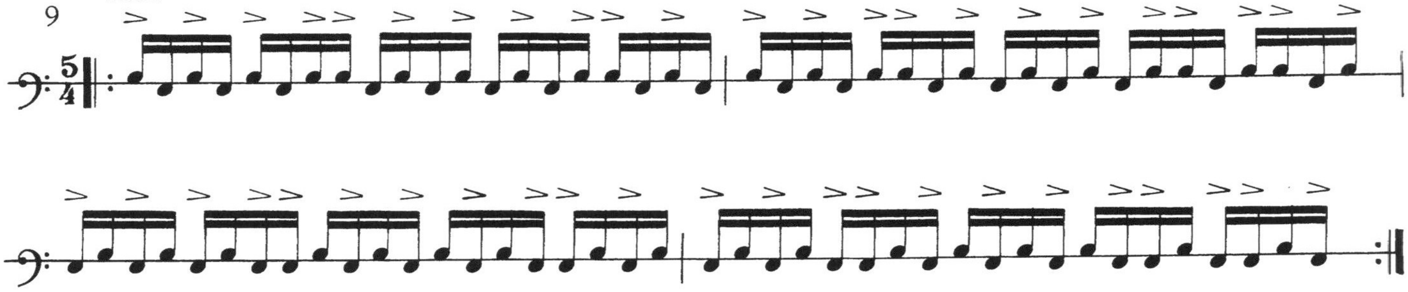
5/4
10 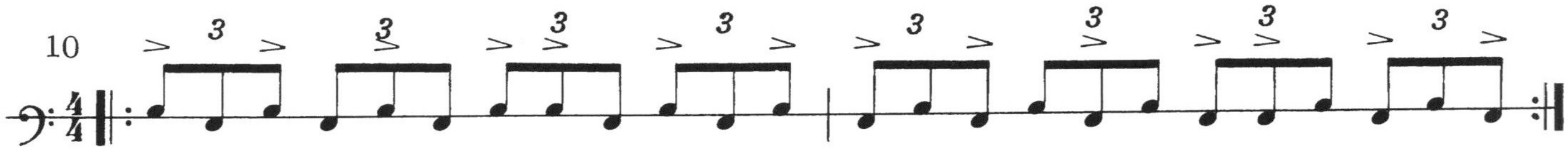
4/4
3
11
ddds 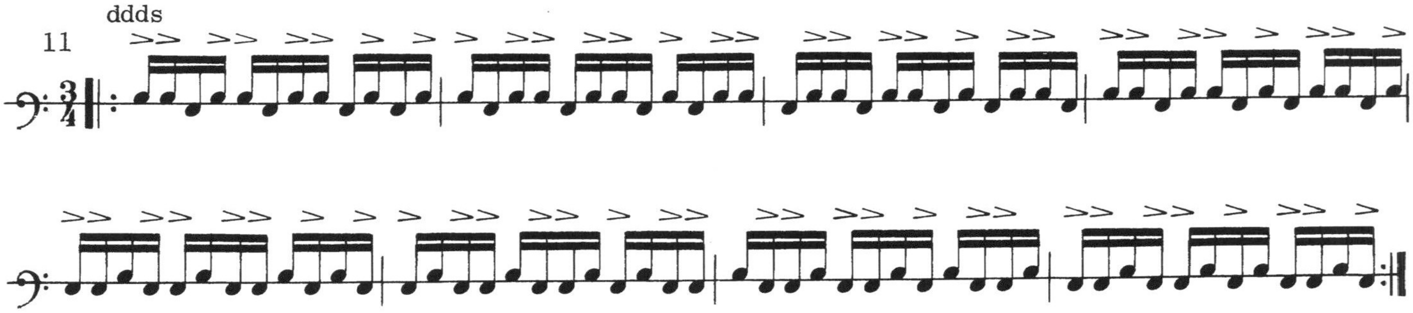
3/4
12
sddd
3/4
3

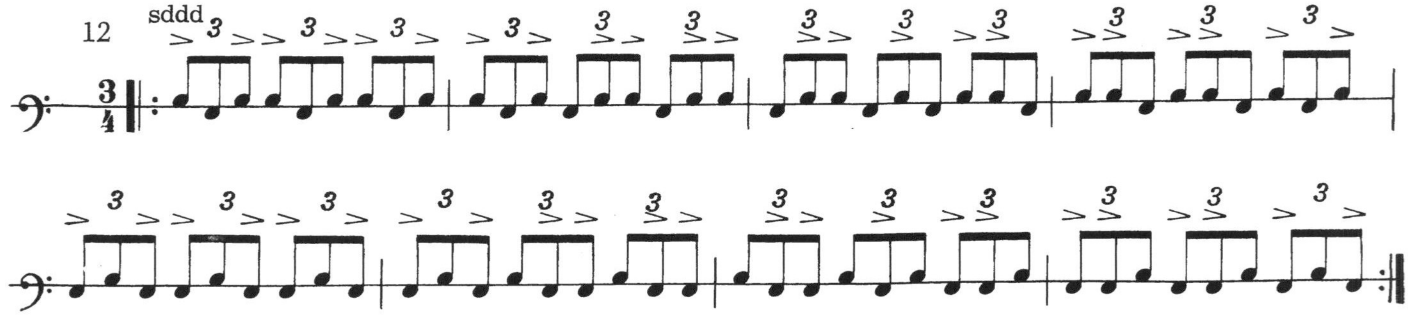

ONE HAND ACCENTING (other hand playing double stroke fill)

DOUBLE STROKE ACCENT BEFORE SINGLE

1. Some of the exercises have suggested ways to play the feet. Create your own foot patterns to supplement the ones suggested by us.

II
R
L
Feet
III
R
L
Feet
IV
R
L
Feet
V
R
L
Feet
one measure exercises
VI
R
L
Feet
VII
R
L
Feet
VIII
R
L
IX
R
L
X
R
F

DOUBLE ACCENT STUDIES

one measure exercises

On all stickings and figures accent 1st of double, 2nd of double, double, 1st of double and double, 2nd cf double and double, just singles, (1st of double, 2nd of double)(single, 1st of double)(single, 2nd of double.)

FIRST AND SECOND BEAT ACCENT ON DOUBLE STROKES

1. Practice each measure separately. 2. Practice as two measure exercises.

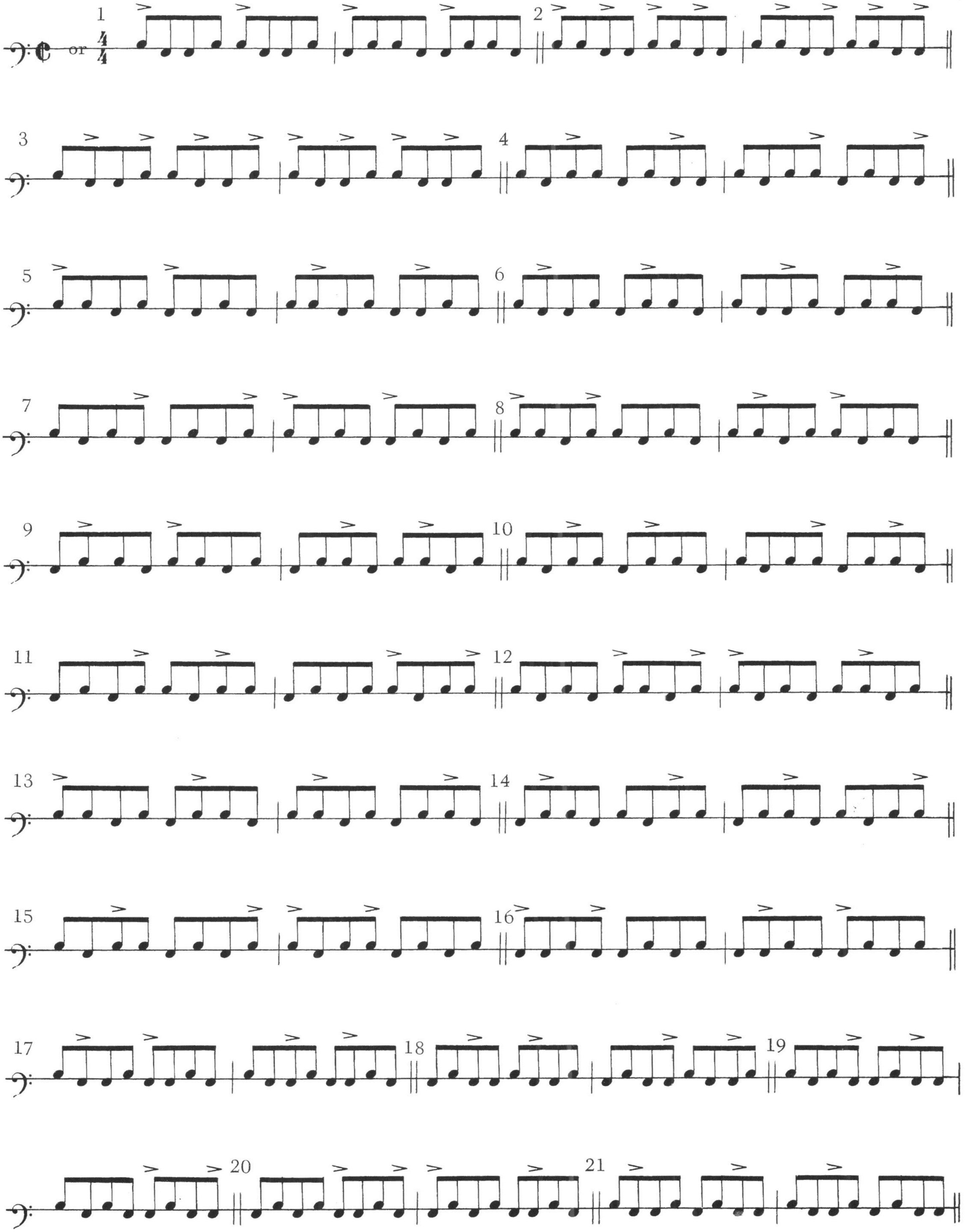

1. Practice each measure separately. 2. Practice as two measure exercises.

ACCENTING IMMEDIATELY AFTER TRIPLE STROKE

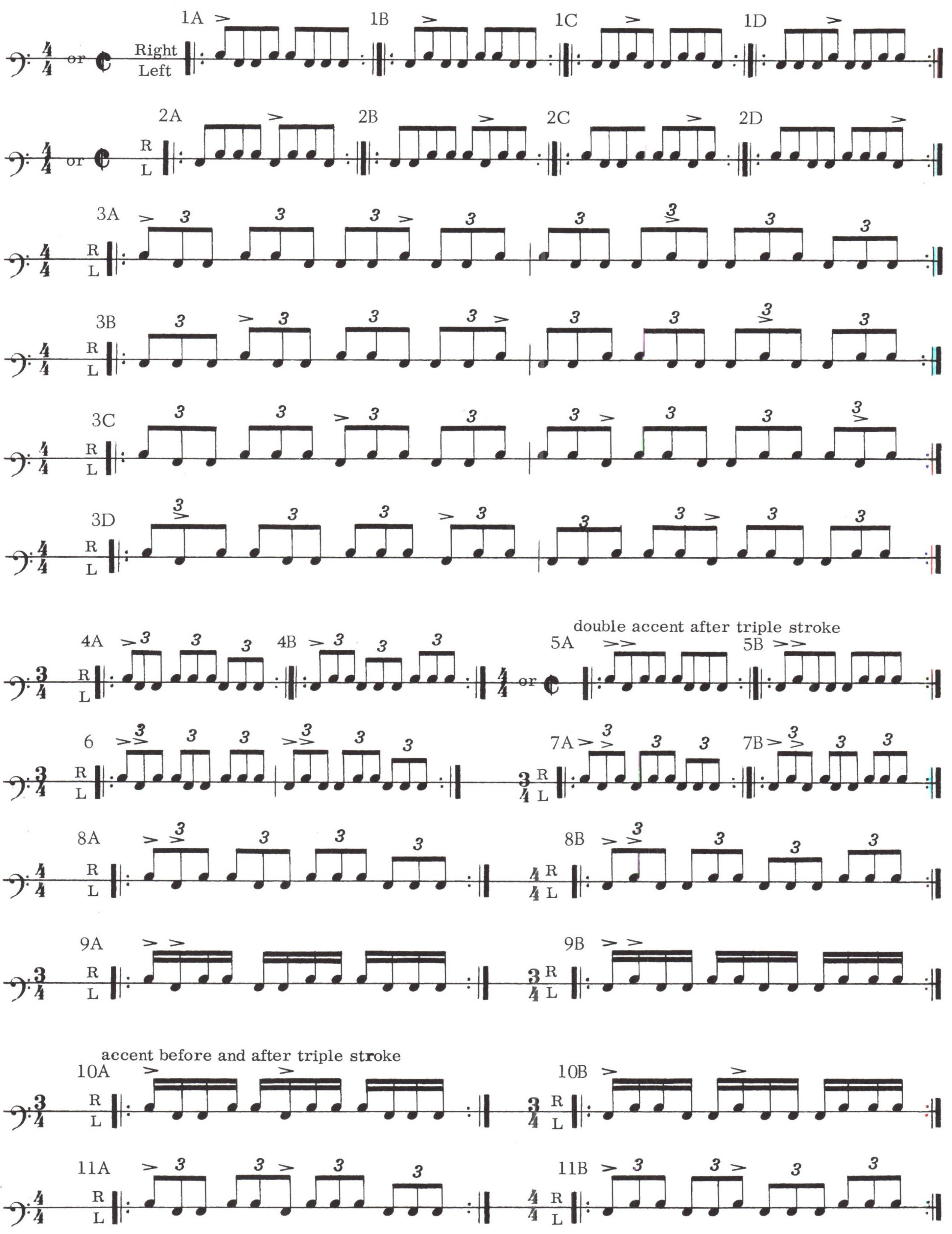

Right
Left
1A 1B 1C 1D
R
L
2A 2B 2C 2D
R
L
3A
R
L
3B
R
L
3C
R
L
3D
R
L
double accent after triple stroke
4A 4B 5A 5B
R
L
6 7A 7B
R
L
8A 8B
R
L
9A 9B
R
L
accent before and after triple stroke
10A 10B
R
L
11A 11B
R
L

ACCENT PHRASES (with fill-ins)

1. Practice each measure separately. 2. Practice in four measure phrases.

ACCENT PHRASES

This page introduces bi-rhythms, in this case TWO AGAINST THREE. (one measure exercises)

3 AGAINST 4

Practice each measure separately before attempting to combine.

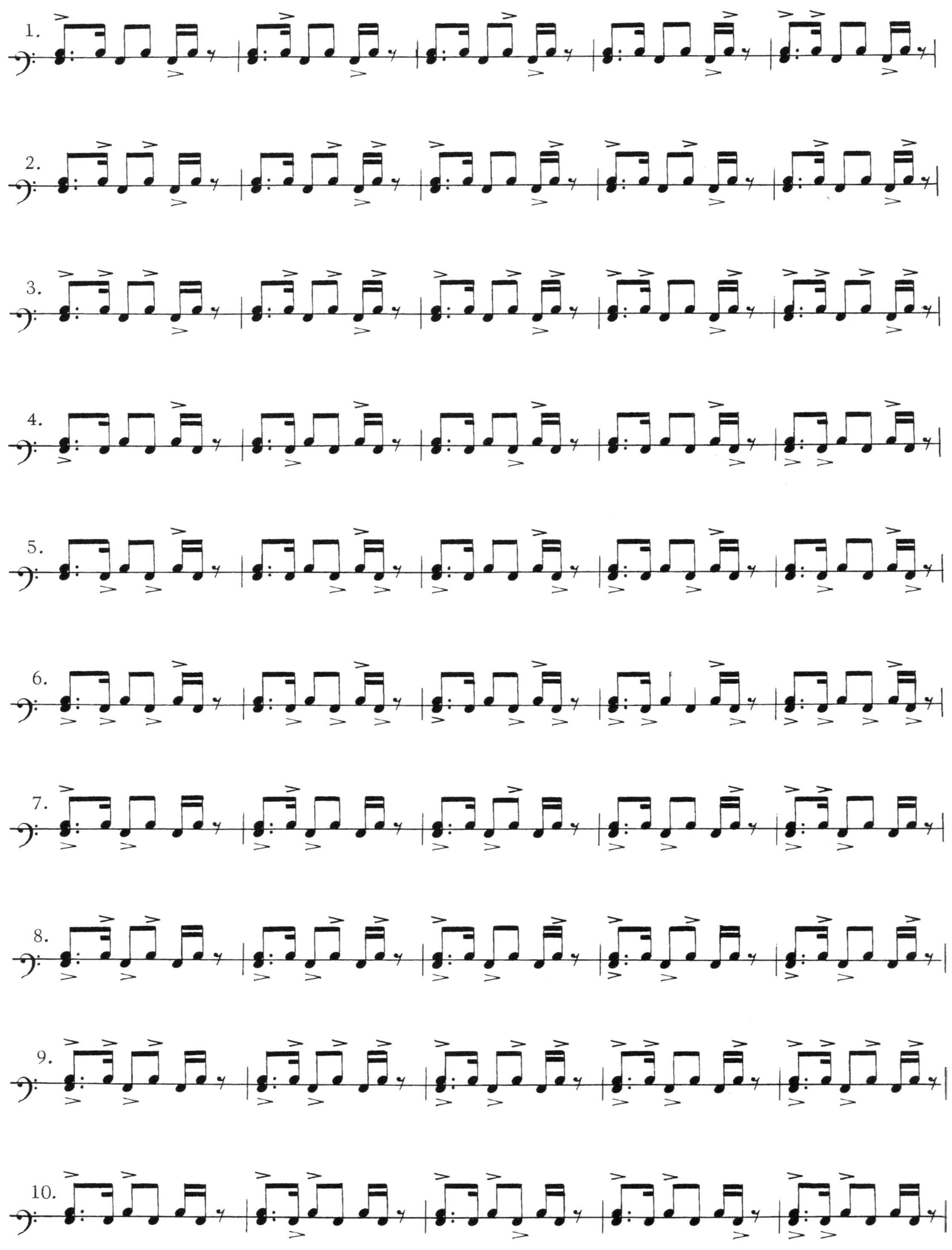

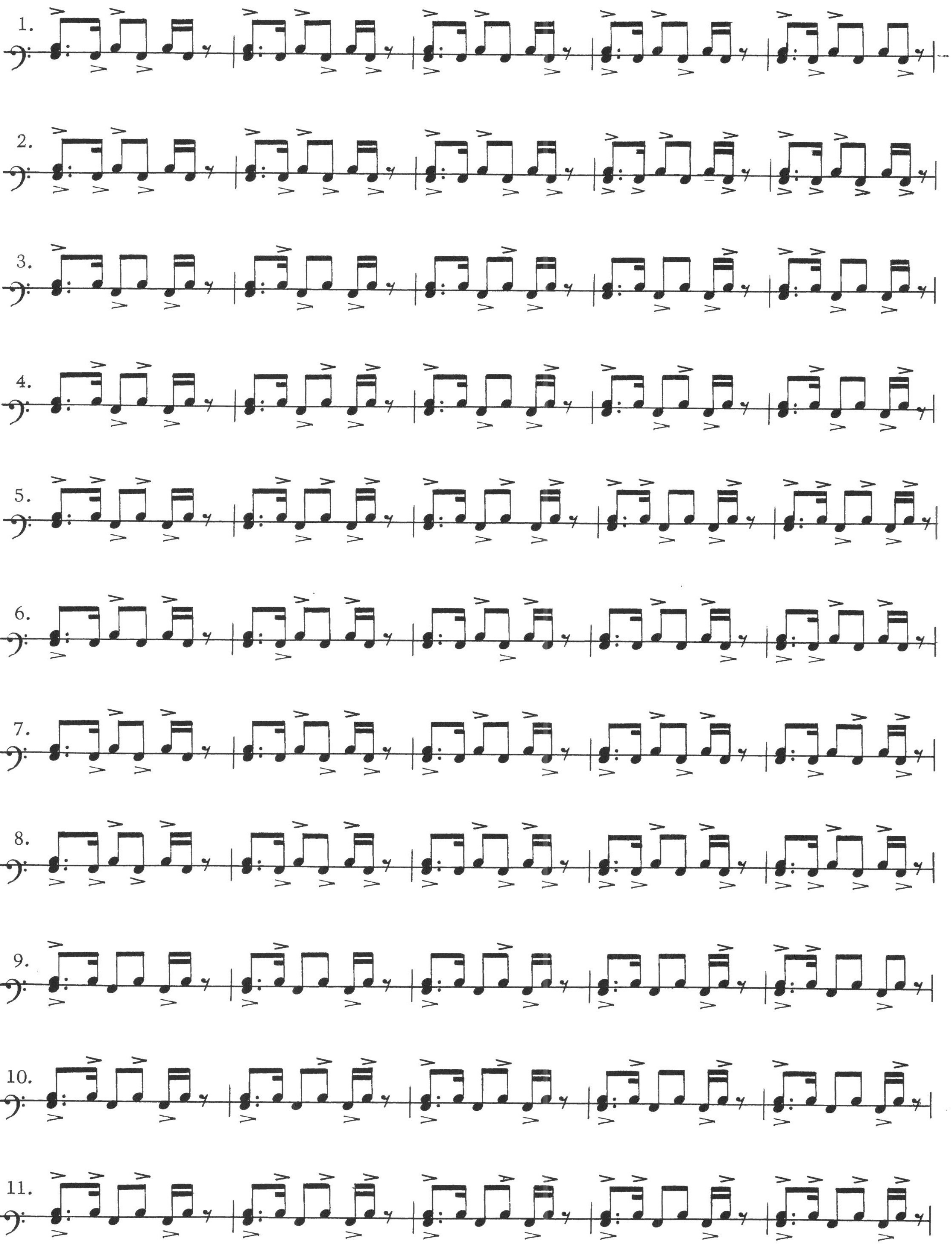

Practice same accent sequences on 5 against 3 and 5 against 4:

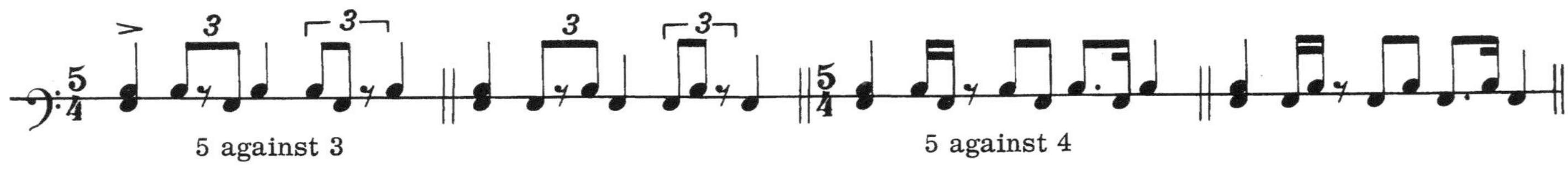

On the following exercises the sticking and accent sequence remains the same, but time signatures and rhythms change.

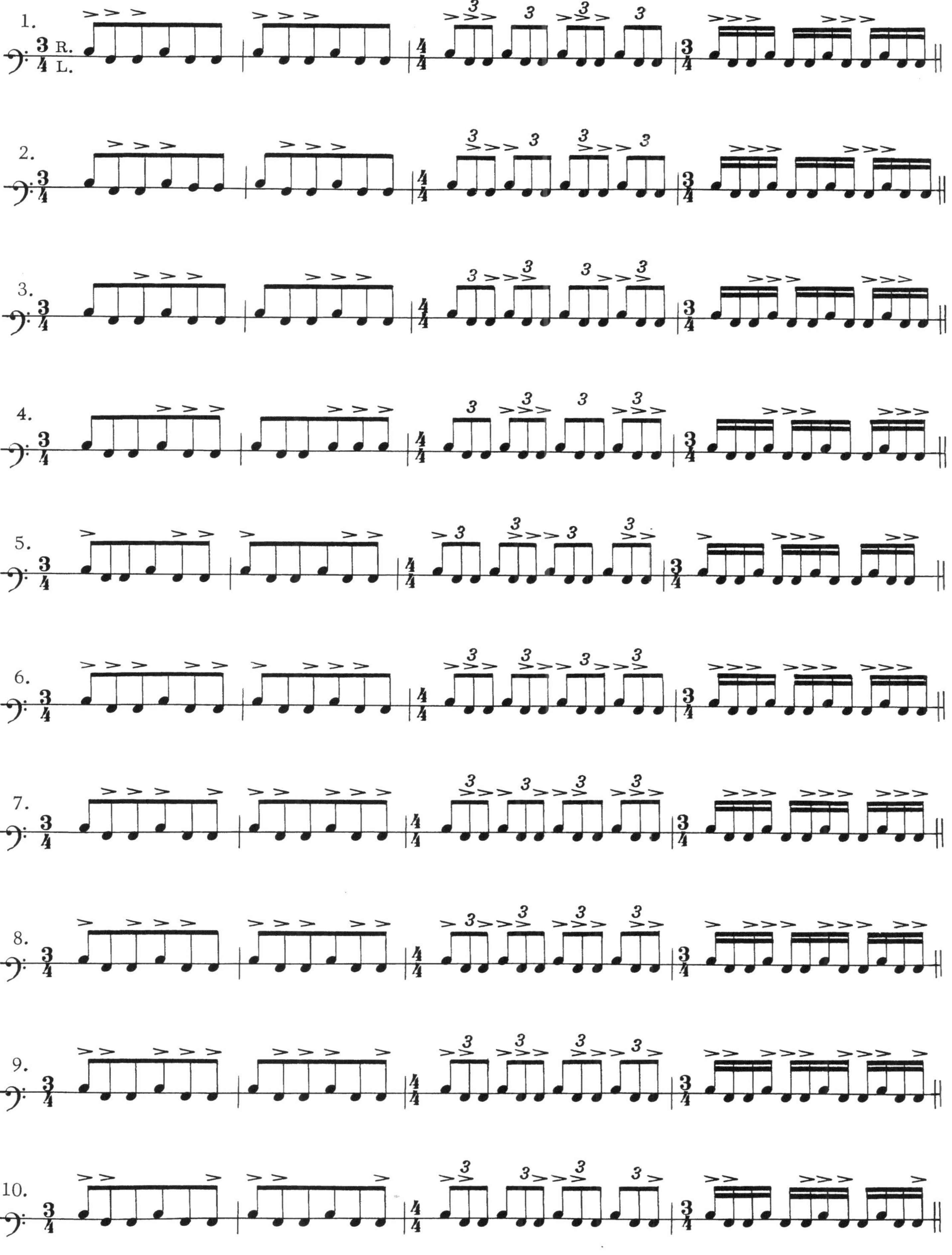

Use the following stickings with the 16 accent patterns on the previous page.

Example: Accent Patterns remain the same:
Sticking changes.

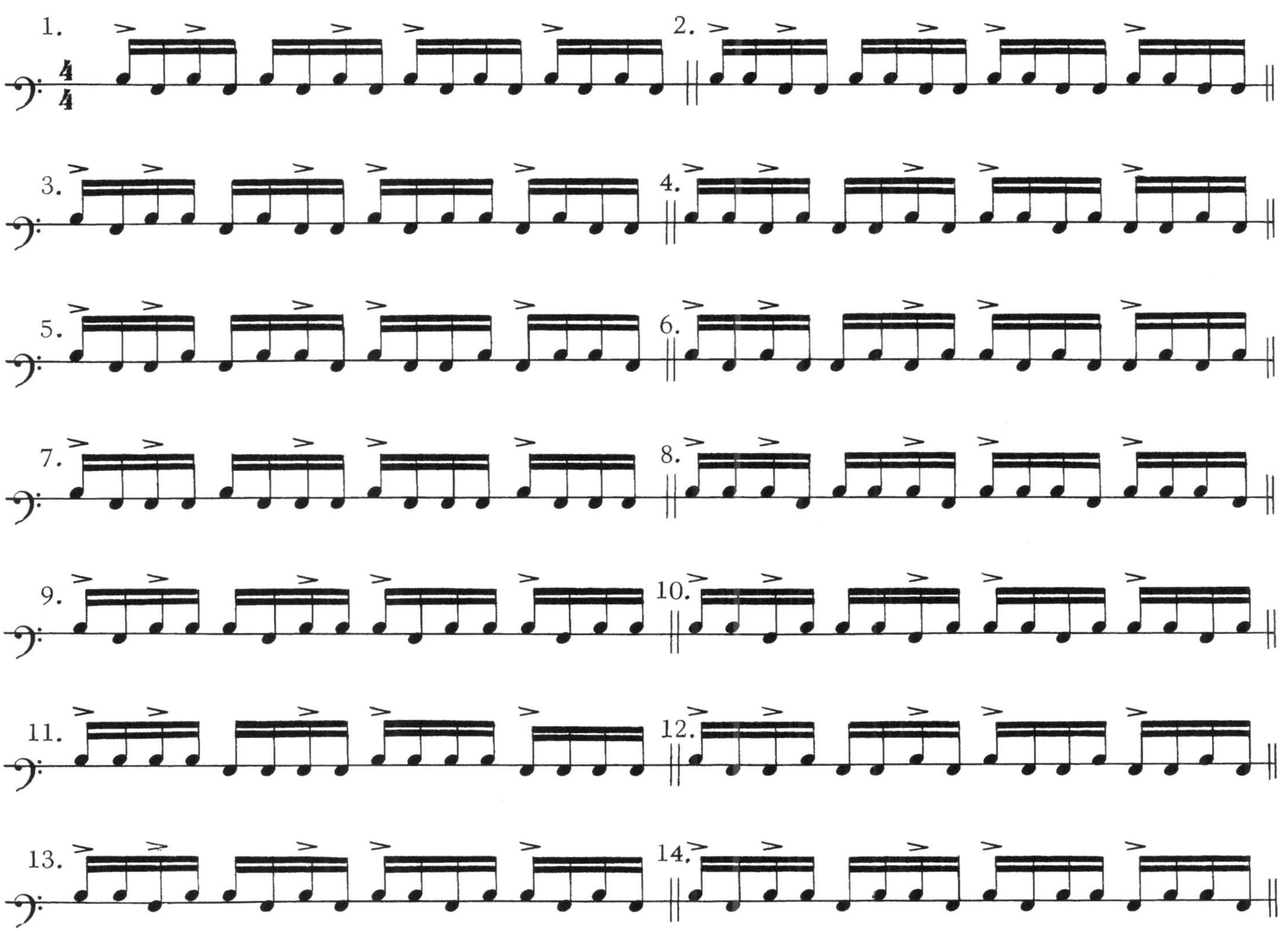

Use the following accent figures with the 14 stickings above; then use your own.

Accent patterns permutate; Sticking remains the same (in this case: Long roll)

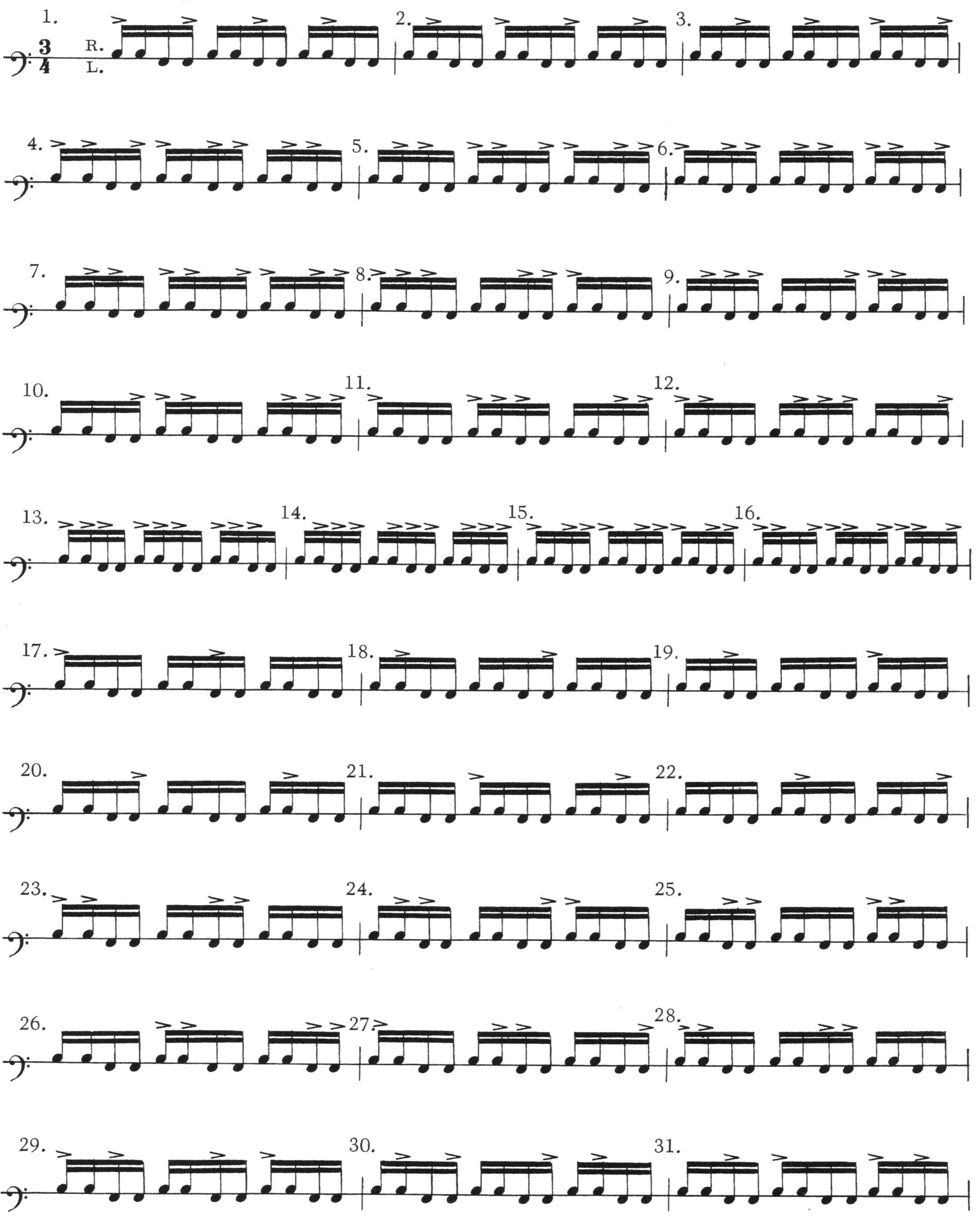

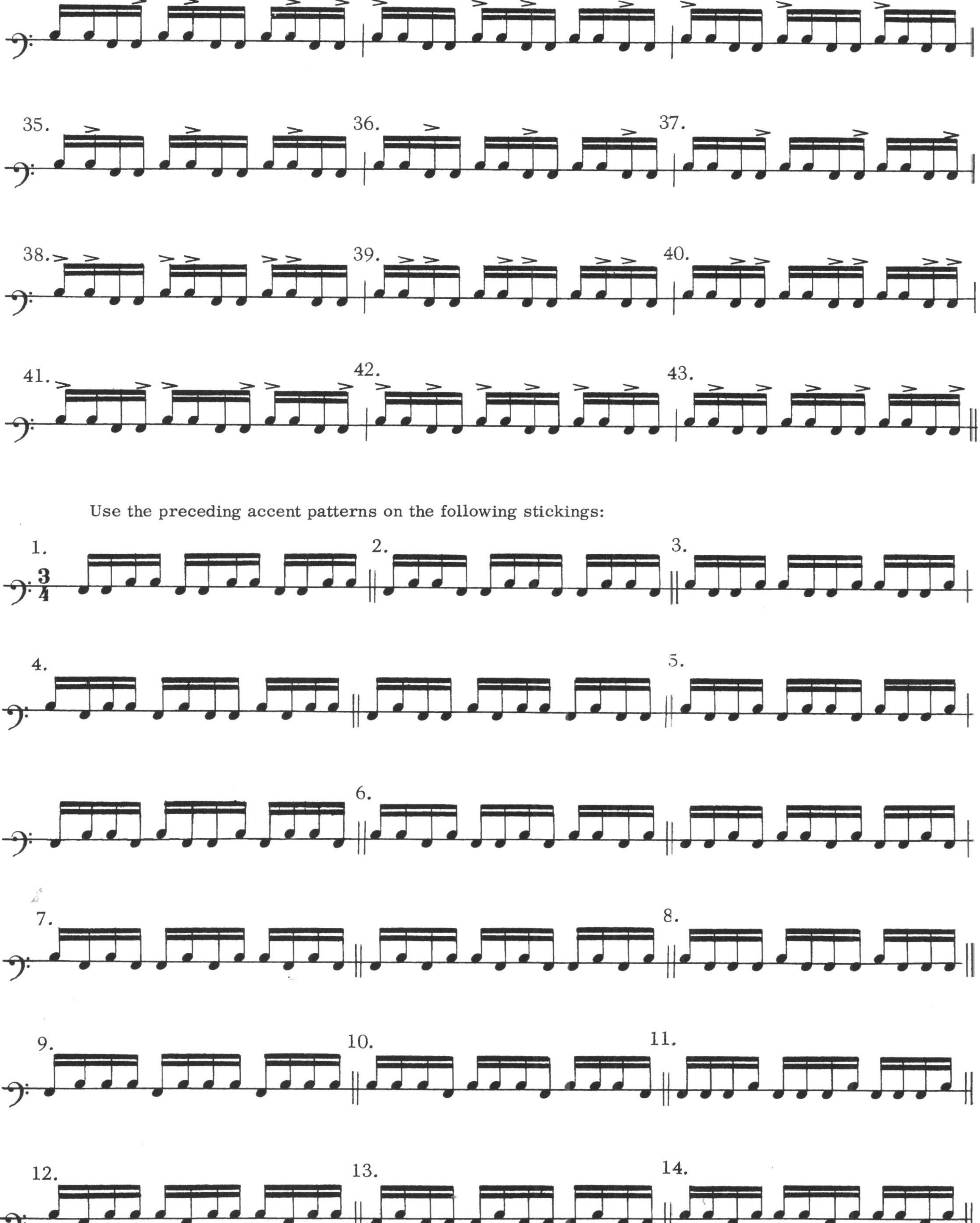

Use the preceding accent patterns on the following stickings:

3 note stickings combined with 2 and 4 note accent patterns:
1. Practice each measure separately.   2. Combine in phrases.

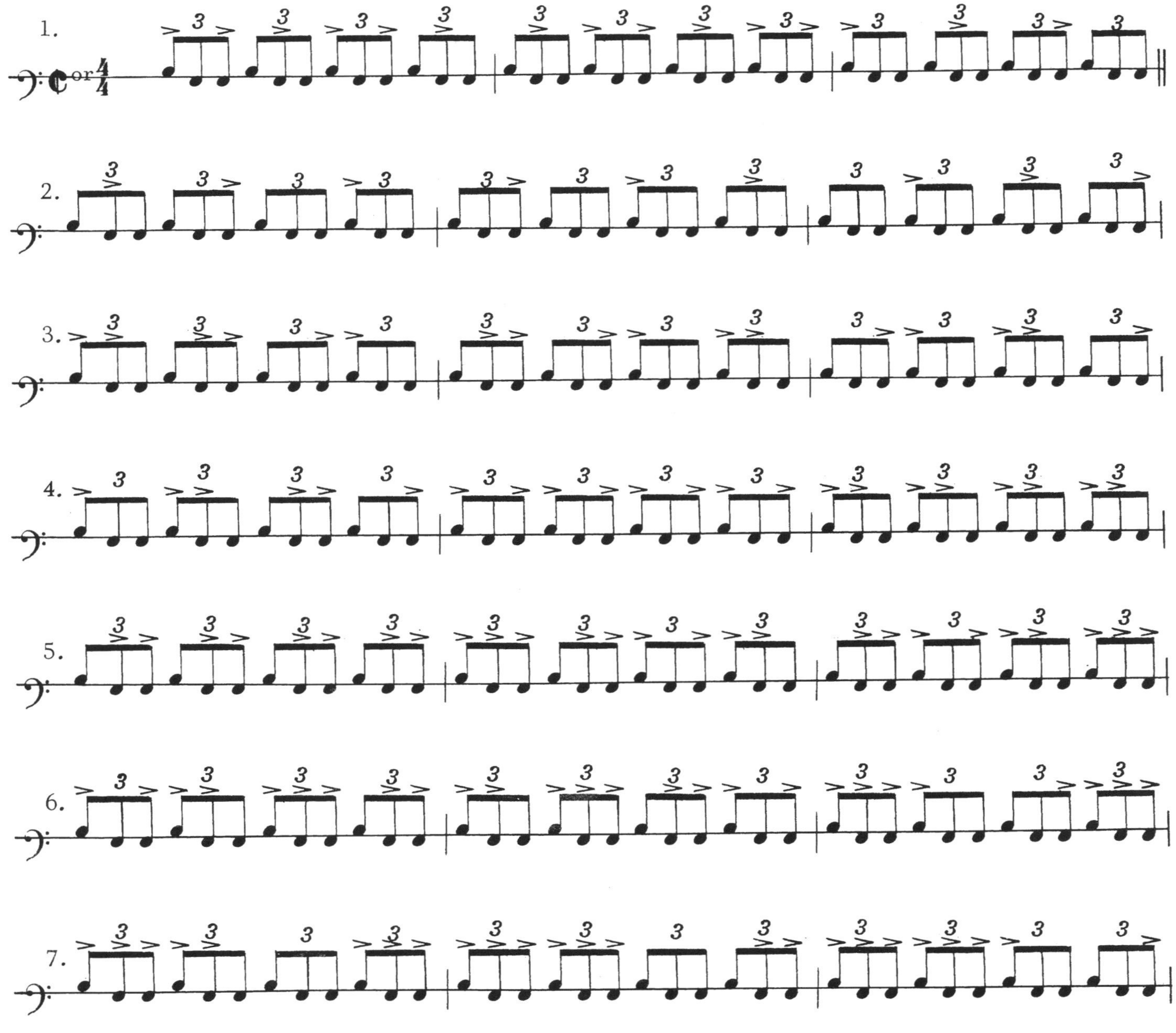

The set of exercises beginning on this page will enable you to gain independent control of accents on harmonic and melodic combinations.

50

HAB 104

STUDIES IN WHICH BOTH THE ACCENTS AND STICKINGS PERMUTATE ON TRIPLETS IN 4/4 TIME

Read down ↓ or across ⟶ ex. accents of 1-12, sticking of A–B–C–D

SUGGESTED ACCENT PATTERNS - ALL STICKINGS

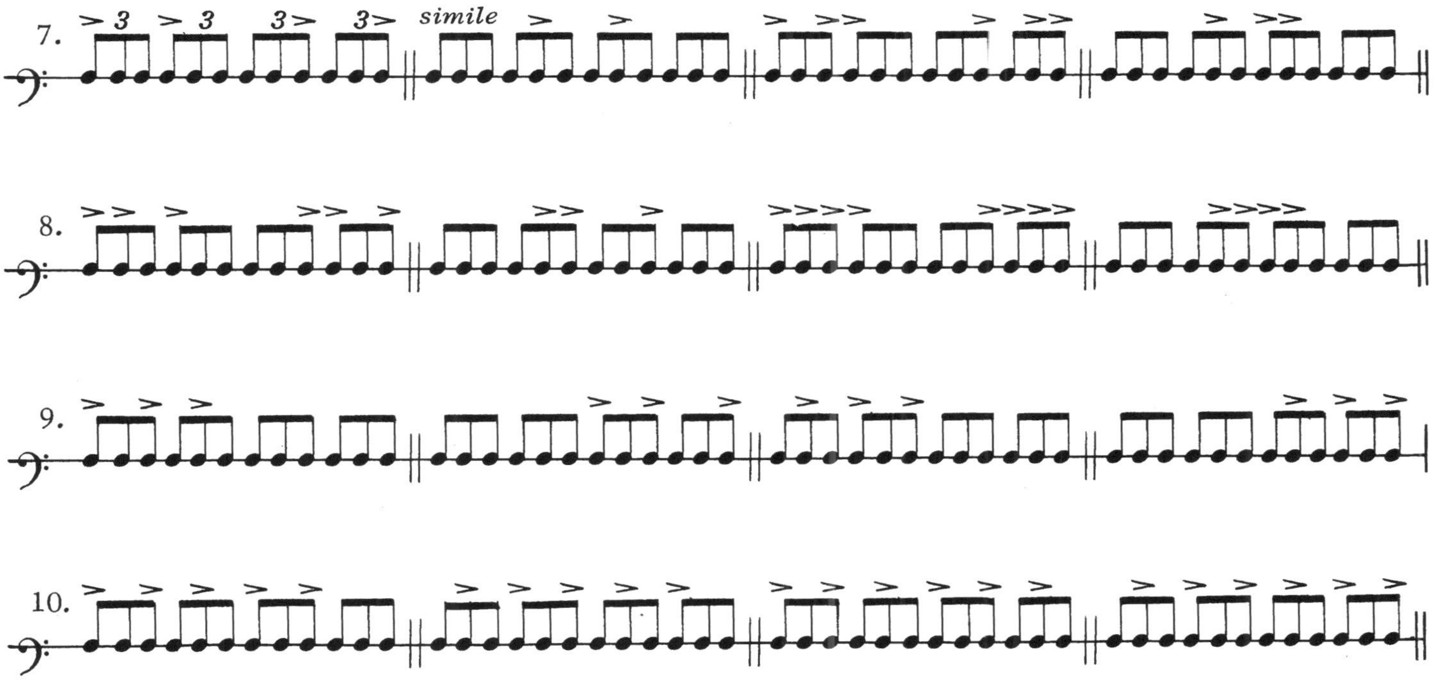

COMBINING DIFFERENT ACCENT PATTERNS

Use all 16 accent patterns in section I with the accent figure and patterns of section II.

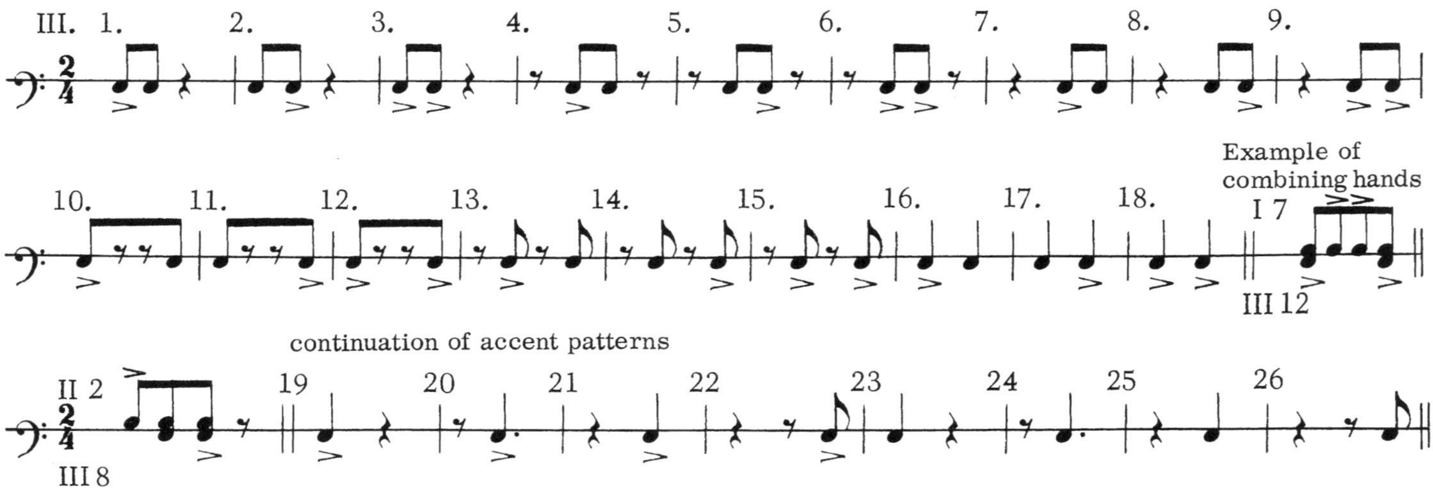

Use all 16 accent patterns in section I with all patterns (26) of section III.

55

Use these stickings with accent patterns in section I on the previous page.

MISCELLANEOUS ACCENTS ON 16th NOTES

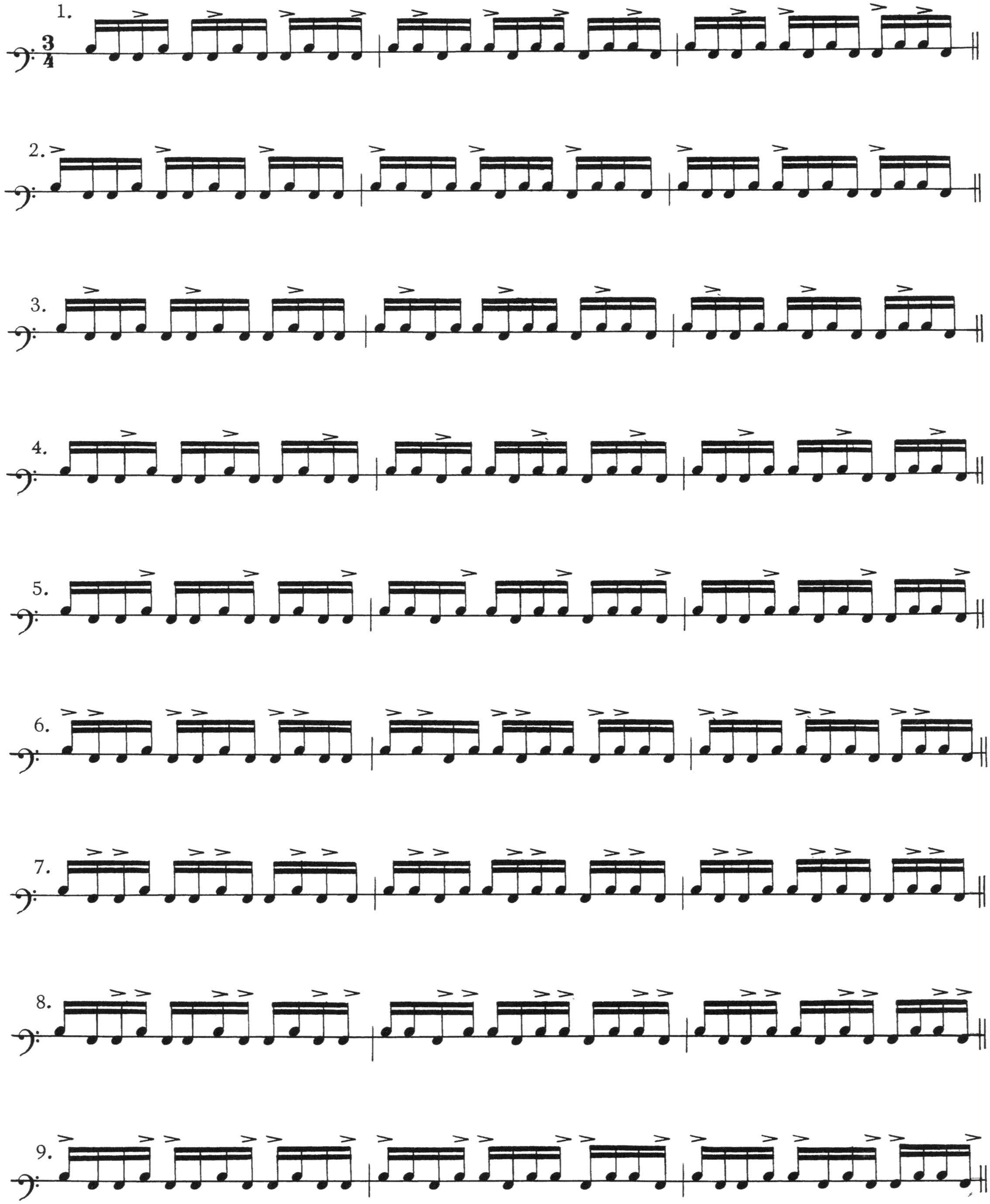

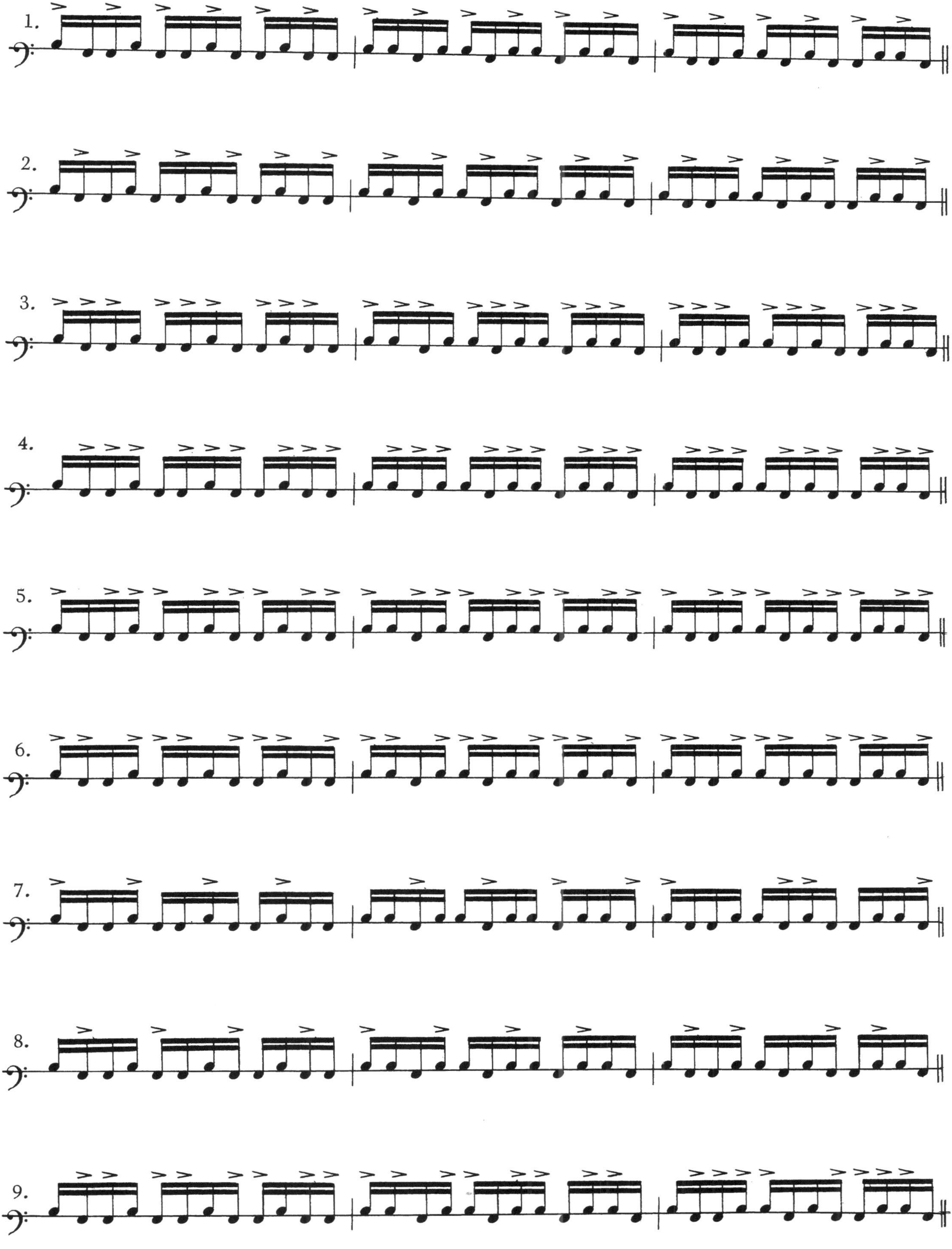

DEGREE OF ACCENTS

Studies to control the strength of accents for better control of dynamics, nuances and inner rhythms.

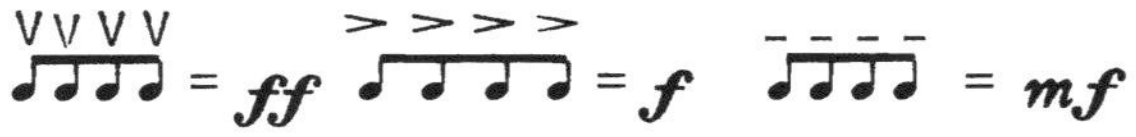

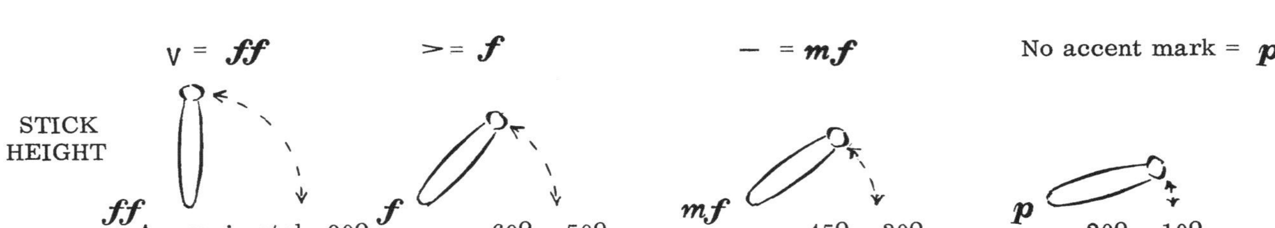

The following examples will help you in controlling the different types of accents:

Use any sticking.

SOLOS

Example 1:

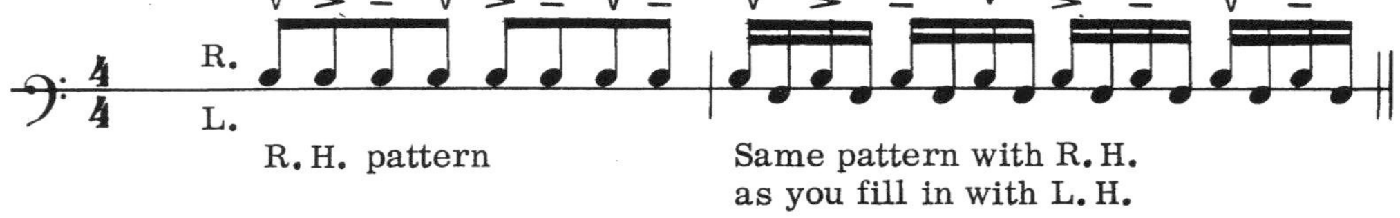

R. H. pattern

Same pattern with R. H. as you fill in with L. H.

Make your own combinations using V > ‒ on all figures and stickings

Example 2:

Example 3:

Example 4:

Combine any of the examples to make a $\frac{3}{4}$ – $\frac{4}{4}$ – $\frac{5}{4}$ or $\frac{6}{4}$ bar

EXAMPLES IN TRIPLET FORM

Use any sticking.

SOLOS

Example 1:

Ex. 2:

Ex. 3:

Ex. 4:

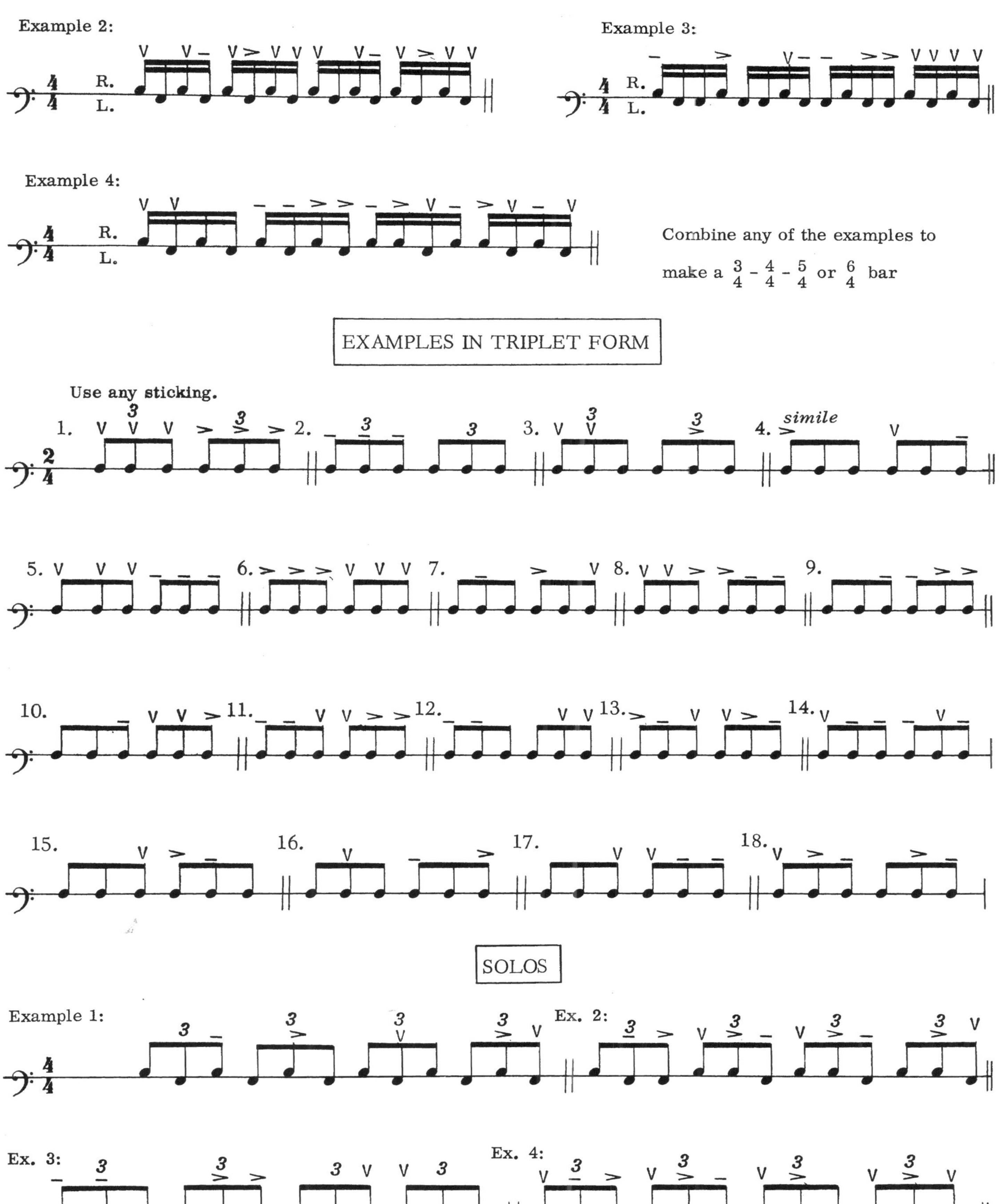